The Noisy Mouse

by June Woodman
Illustrated by Ken Morton

D0576775

BRIMAX BOOKS · NEWMARKET · ENGLAND

Mouse is very little.
She has a little nose,
two bright little eyes
and four little pink feet.
But she has a VERY BIG VOICE!
When she sings and bangs
her drum she makes
a VERY LOUD NOISE!

One day Mouse makes up a new song. "Boom, Boom, Boom," goes her drum. "I can play on the big bass drum," she sings very loudly. "Yes," says Mouse, to herself. "That's just right for the Parade." She wants to try the song on her friends.

She marches off to find them.
Ostrich is picking flowers.
"Listen to this, Ostrich!"
shouts Mouse. She begins to
bang on her drum and she sings,
"I can play on the big bass . . ."
"Ooooh!" moans Ostrich.
"You make my ears ache!"
She hides her head in her
bucket and runs away.

Mouse goes marching on.
Lion is sleeping in his den.
He is wearing a flower necklace.
"Listen to this, Lion!" shouts
Mouse. She begins to sing.
"I can play on the big . . ."
Lion jumps up, banging his
head on the roof.
"Aaaarrr," roars Lion. "You
make my head ache!" He puts
his paws over his ears.

Mouse marches to Hippo's pool. She sees Hippo and Alligator. "Listen to this, you two!" shouts Mouse. "I can play on the . . ." Alligator jumps up with a start. He sinks his teeth into Hippo. "Eeeeeee," cries Alligator. "You make my teeth ache!" "Aieeeee," cries Hippo. "You make my . . ." Mouse runs off before Hippo can finish.

Mouse goes marching on.
Giraffe is picking flowers
from the top of the vines.
"Listen to this, Giraffe!"
shouts Mouse. "I can play on . . ."
Giraffe looks down at her.
"Oh! You make my neck ache,
Mouse," says Giraffe.

Mouse goes marching on.
Kangaroo is washing Baby.
"Listen to this, Kangaroo,"
shouts Mouse. "I can play . . ."
Kangaroo gives a jump and
drops Baby. He falls
in the water – SPLASH!

"Ow," cries Baby Kangaroo. "You make my tail ache." "You are too noisy, Mouse," says Kangaroo. "Try to play quietly. Put this sponge on your drumsticks. And sing in a whisper."

"I'll try!" shouts Mouse.

"The Parade is starting!
The Parade is starting!"
squawks Parrot. Elephant
is in charge.
"Get into line!" he says.
The animals all line up.
There are flowers everywhere
for the great Flower Parade.

"Lead on, Mouse!" orders Elephant. The Parade sets off with Mouse at the front.
She begins to play the drum. "Tap, tap, tap," goes the drum very quietly. Mouse whispers, "I can play on the big bass drum.'
"What did you say, Mouse?" asks Giraffe.

Spider misses a beat and bumps into Ostrich. She drops her bucket. Alligator trips over it. Monkey steps on Lion's tail and Lion grabs at Kangaroo. Baby falls out of her pouch and everyone ends up in a heap. What a mess!

"Oh dear! Oh dear!" cries Parrot.
"We can't hear the beat!"
complains Hippo.
"We can't keep in step!"
cries Spider.
"It's all my fault," says Kangaroo.
"Make as much noise as you
can, Mouse."
"Yippeeeee!" cries Mouse.

So they all line up again.
"Boom, Boom, Boom,"
goes the drum.
Noisy Mouse starts to sing,
"I can play on the big bass drum.
And this is the music to it.
Boom, Boom, BOOM!
goes the big bass drum.
THAT'S the way to do it!"
What a great Flower Parade!
WHAT a noisy Mouse!

Here are some words in the story.

bright	ache
voice	washing
noise	whisper
bass	charge
parade	everywhere
marches	heap
moans	line